Lia's
Fabulous Tutus

written by Cynthia Lilly and Michael Miller

illustrated by Sona Jacob and Jacob Nicholas

Fulton Books
Meadville, PA

Published by Fulton Books 2022

ISBN 979-8-88505-032-6 (hardcover)
ISBN 979-8-88505-031-9 (digital)

Printed in the United States of America

DEDICATION

To my mother, Ruby Lilly.

This book is in honor of you because I have so many wonderful memories that I just can't keep to myself. Your purity, love, grace, wisdom, and light will always live on within me and everyone you crossed paths with. You are now my precious guardian angel.

Love you always...my sweetmeat.

—Cynthia Lilly

Lia woke up her brother, Nate, every morning to help her practice dancing to become a fabulous ballerina.

Even while brushing their teeth,
Lia danced circles around Nate.

4

Lia danced in her pretty tutu while
she and Nate made breakfast
with their grandmother, Mema.

Lia danced in her pretty tutu while she practiced her 123s and ABCs. Mema would say, "Now, Lia, there's a time and place for everything."

8

Every day, Lia would do extra chores around the house so she could fill up her piggy bank with the money Mema gives her to buy a fabulous tutu.

Lia saved enough money and wanted to surprise her brother, Nate, with a gift. Nate opened his eyes, and to his surprise, it was a tutu. Everyone burst out laughing, especially Mema, as Nate did not expect to receive a tutu as a gift.

13

Lia danced in the bathtub as the bubbles formed a tutu around her. Mema sat back and laughed with delight.

Now it was time for bed. Lia still wanted to dance, but she remembered what Mema told her, *There's a time and place for everything*, as she fell asleep into her dreams of being a fabulous ballerina.

16

THE END